Little Swan

by
Jonathan London

illustrated by
Kristina Rodanas

Marshall Cavendish Children

The first thing Ko-hoh saw when he cracked through the eggshell was his mother and father towering over him.

Then he saw three swan chicks,
scrawny and confused,
crying *peep! peep! peep!*

Ko-hoh settled down with the others
beneath his mother's soft, warm feathers.

Two days later,
the babies slid out of their nest
and into the lake.

Their parents tipped bottoms up,
bicycling their feet for balance,
snaking their long necks deep,
stirring up a watery salad
for the little ones to nibble.

Ten days later, Ko-hoh and the others
tipped their bottoms up
for the first time,
and tried to feed on their own.

They kicked in the air
and flailed and swayed . . .
and toppled over—*splash!*
Duckweed dangled from their bills.

When ravens and eagles swooped above
and pike and turtles swam below,
Ko-hoh climbed aboard his mother's back,
where he felt safe.

It was the season of the cygnets —
the season when the parents' flight feathers
fell out, so they couldn't fly.

All summer, the family swam together
and stayed together.
They pulled roots and shoots
from the riverbanks,

ate snails in the grass,
and dove back into the water
to nibble on reeds and water moss
and pond lilies.

In this way, the young grew quickly.
And as summer turned into fall,
the parents' flight feathers grew back —
and the flight feathers on the cygnets
grew in.

They were ready to learn to fly!
Ko-hoh hopped . . .
and flopped . . .
and stumbled and fell.

But soon he was running on water,
and taking off with the others
on low flights over the marshes.

Every day, they flew a little farther.
And every day, the weather grew colder.
Ice formed along the edges of the lakes.

Before the lakes froze over,
the swans would have to fly south
for the winter.

But one day, just before dawn,
a young, hungry grizzly came crashing down
through the willows and the ice.
He charged toward Ko-hoh.

Ko-hoh-h-h! Ko-hoh-h-h!
trumpeted his parents.
Ko-hoh-h-h! Ko-hoh-h-h!

With fierce strong blows,
they swung their wings like clubs.
Ko-hoh flapped and squeaked
like a broken whistle.

At last, the startled bear
scrambled off into the rosy mist,
and disappeared.

Ko-hoh was safe.

But the lake was freezing over.
Heads bobbing, restless to go,
the swan family called to each other.
It was time.

Time to migrate!

They banded together,
and in single file,
ran on water . . .

and took to the air.

With a graceful, majestic power
they formed a V
and flew high, high
in the sky-kingdom of the swan,
honking *ko-hoh-h-h! ko-hoh-h-h!*

Ko-hoh and his family
would wing back in the spring.
Someday, he would have a family
of his own.

A NOTE FROM THE AUTHOR

The trumpeter swans of this story are the largest waterfowl in the world. They weigh up to forty pounds and have a wingspan of eight feet.

Trumpeter swans mate for life. They breed in the spring and build huge nests, often on top of beaver or muskrat lodges in the northern lakes and marshes of North America. In April or May, the female lays one large white egg every other day until there are three to seven eggs. While the mother sits on the eggs, the father stands guard and protects the eggs against bears, otters, and other intruders. After thirty-five days, the eggs hatch and the fragile babies (cygnets) are born.

Swans fiercely protect their young, flapping their wings like clubs if a predator draws near. They have been known to chase away bears and to break the legs of men who have come too close. The Kootenai Indians named the swans' call "ko-hoh," after the horn-like blast made by the birds while migrating or when alarmed.

Young trumpeters stay with their parents until their return migration in the spring. At age three or four, they start families of their own.

Once common in North America, the swans became almost extinct in the United States by the 1930s because of hunting and the loss of marshland. Thanks to the efforts of naturalists who have worked to restore and protect swans in the wild, these majestic symbols of beauty, grace, and power have survived to this day to fill the skies with their cries—*Ko-hoh-h-h! Ko-hoh!*

For Jon of Alaska
—J.L.

For Carol Nickerson, thank you
—K.R.

Library of Congress Cataloging-in-Publication Data
London, Jonathan.
Little swan / by Jonathan London ; illustrated by Kristina Rodanas.
— 1st ed.
p. cm.
Summary: A trumpeter swan family stays close together as the cygnets learn how to feed themselves, honk when predators are nearby, and develop flight feathers. Includes facts about the trumpeter swan, the largest waterfowl in the world.
ISBN 978-0-7614-5523-3
1. Trumpeter swan—Juvenile fiction. [1. Trumpeter swan—Fiction.
2. Swans—Fiction. 3. Animals—Infancy—Fiction.]
I. Rodanas, Kristina, ill.
II. Title.
PZ10.3.L8534Li 2009
[E]—dc22
2008009246

Text copyright © 2009 by Jonathan London
Illustrations copyright © 2009 by Kristina Rodanas

The illustrations were rendered in colored pencil over watercolor wash.
Book design by Vera Soki
Editor: Margery Cuyler

Printed in Malaysia
First edition
1 3 5 6 4 2

mc Marshall Cavendish
Children